# THE PIRATE GIRL'S TREASURE

## AN ORIGAMI ADVENTURE

PEYTON LEUNG · HILARY LEUNG



Kids Can Press

For all grandparents — P.L. & H.L.

Kids Can Press acknowledges the financial support of the Government of Ontario, through the Ontario Media Development Corporation's Ontario Book Initiative; the Ontario Arts Council; the Canada Council for the Arts; and the Government of Canada, through the BPIDP, for our publishing activity.

Published in Canada by
Kids Can Press Ltd.
25 Dockside Drive
Toronto, ON M5A 0B5

Published in the U.S. by
Kids Can Press Ltd.
2250 Military Road
Tonawanda, NY 14150

www.kidscanpress.com

The text is set in Tempus Sans.

Edited by Yvette Ghione
Designed by Hilary Leung and Julia Naimska

This book is smyth sewn casebound.
Manufactured in Singapore, in 10/2011 by Tien Wah Press (Pte) Ltd.

CM 12 0 9 8 7 6 5 4 3 2 1

Library and Archives Canada Cataloguing in Publication

Leung, Peyton, 1978–
The pirate girl's treasure : an origami adventure / written by Peyton Leung ; illustrated by Hilary Leung.

ISBN 978-1-55453-660-3

I. Leung, Hilary II. Title.

PS8623.E9355P57 2012 jC813'.6 C2011-904884-1

Kids Can Press is a Corus™ Entertainment company

Ahoy, matey! I was inspired to write this story by an origami model known as "The Captain's Shirt," which is a traditional paper-folding design that transforms a boat into a T-shirt. In this book, a sequence of folds is told as a tale of daring and adventure that will help you remember the steps to create your own captain's shirt or, in this case, *pirate's* shirt! Happy reading and folding — may all your models be ship-shape!

— Peyton Leung

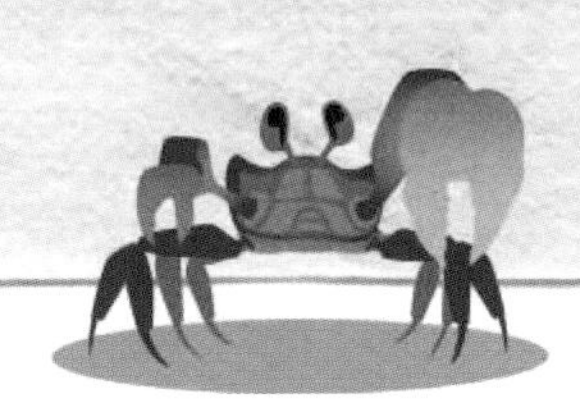

Once upon a time, there was a pirate girl who, like her pirate grandfather, sailed the seven seas. One day, she received an unusual letter from him that read:

*Granddaughter, I have journeyed far and seen many treasures. If you follow the map below, you will find a special treasure that I have hidden for you.*

The pirate girl clapped her hands with delight — she couldn't wait to see what her grandfather had left for her, but even more exciting was the thought of a new adventure!

The pirate girl studied her grandfather's map carefully. She folded the map in half and then in half again, making sure all the corners met evenly, and tucked it carefully into her pocket. Then, with a skip to her step, she set out to find the treasure.

First, the pirate girl came to a very tall mountain. She had never climbed one before, but she was always keen to challenge herself, and she was doubly inspired by the quest her grandfather had set for her.

She climbed up along the main ridge of the mountain, and though it was steep and treacherous, she made it all the way to the top.

Resting at the summit, she paused to look at the land below. She could see all the way to the sea, where the treasure island was marked with a big black *X* on the map. Her spirits buoyed, the pirate girl climbed down the other side of the mountain.

When she reached the bottom, the pirate girl gazed up in awe at the grand mountain that had offered such an amazing view.

Next, the pirate girl went down
into the valley at the base of
the mountain.

This valley led to another valley
at the foot of another mountain.
All the while, the sun blazed
overhead.

Feeling hot under the sun's dazzling rays, the pirate girl paused to put on her trusty pirate's hat. But even with the hat shading her, the girl was growing tired from the relentless heat. Still, slowly and steadily, she walked on. *I must keep going to find Grandfather's treasure!* she thought.

Soon the pirate girl came to a cave.

Eager to escape the heat, she rushed inside. But because her eyes were not used to the darkness, the pirate girl tripped on a rock!

Luckily, she was not hurt, so she picked herself up and moved carefully through the dark cave. When at last the pirate girl saw daylight up ahead, she started to hurry again — and tripped on another rock!

With a sigh, she picked herself up once more and made her way out of the cave extra carefully.

Outside the cave, the pirate girl found herself on a beach. *How will I get to the island?* she wondered, stretching out her arms and looking to the sky for the answer.

Then, just out of the corner of her eye, she noticed a small boat! It wasn't a pirate ship, but it would do.

The boat looked like it had been beached for some time, but the pirate girl checked it over and found it was still seaworthy.

She launched the boat and soon was out in the middle of the sea.

The pirate girl had just spotted the treasure island when she noticed dark clouds gathering on the horizon. Trouble was brewing, and the pirate girl felt small and vulnerable in her little boat.

The wind started gusting,
and the waves rose higher and higher.
With a flash of lightning and a crack of
thunder, rain began pouring down from the
sky. Then, a bolt of lightning struck the center of the
boat! There was no time to be scared — the pirate girl
gripped the oars tightly and started rowing hard for the island.

No sooner had she taken a few strokes than a shark lunged out of the water and bit off the boat's stern! The pirate girl gave a startled cry, then grabbed a bucket and began bailing water as fast as she could.

But suddenly, the boat was picked up by a huge wave and sent crashing down bow first onto a reef — the pirate girl had to abandon ship!

The pirate girl knew there was nothing to do but swim for land, and she struggled to stay afloat in the stormy sea. She had only one thought in mind: *I won't give up on Grandfather's treasure!*

By the time she finally came ashore, the storm had passed and the sun was shining once again. The pirate girl slowly took in her surroundings. Scanning the beach, she saw an *X* marking a spot nearby — she had made it to the treasure island! She ran over and started digging.

Soon the pirate girl's fingers tapped on something solid — a treasure chest! With a triumphant shout, she pulled it out of the sand and opened it.

Inside she found a neatly folded bundle with a note on top:

*Granddaughter, congratulations on making the journey and finding your treasure! May you always wear this pirate's shirt with pride! With love, Grandfather.*

The pirate girl gently unfolded the shirt
and pulled it on over her head.

And the pirate girl smiled, knowing that she was a brave and capable pirate just like her grandfather and that many more amazing adventures awaited her!

Yo ho, adventurer! Ready to set out on your own quest? Follow these instructions carefully to retrace the steps of the pirate girl's journey — treasure awaits you, too!

1. Start with a rectangular piece of paper — your map! — positioned lengthwise.

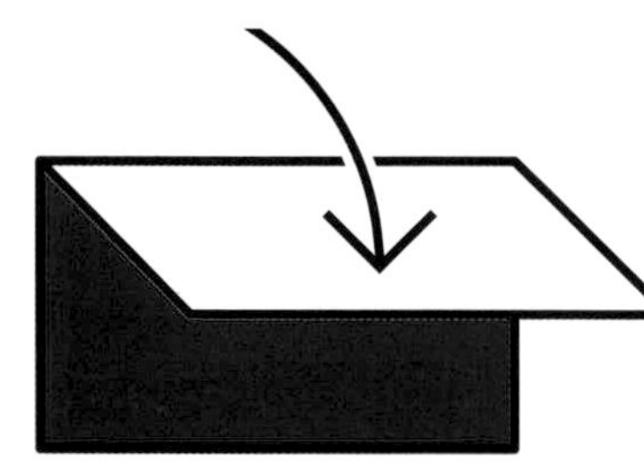

2. Fold the paper toward you in half.

3. Fold the paper in half again, toward the left.

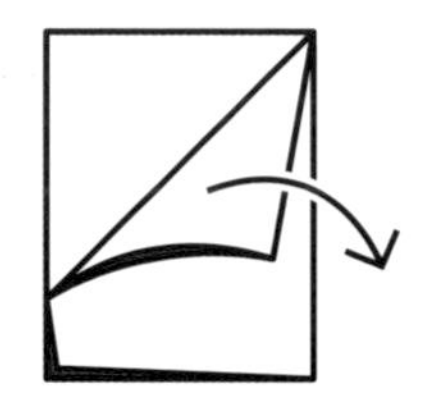

4. Fold the top folded edge down to line up with the right side, creating a triangle above a rectangle (go up the mountain).

5. Turn the model over. Fold the top folded edge down to line up with the left side (go down the mountain).

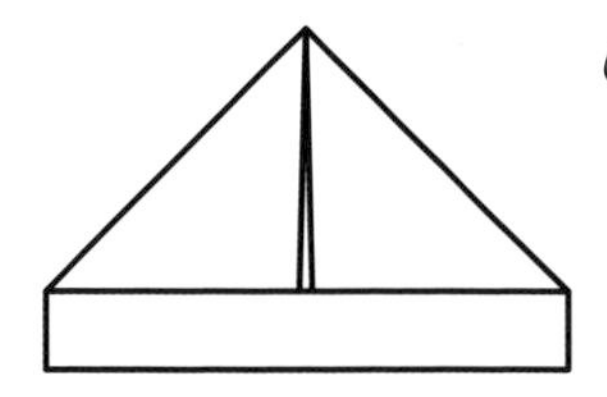

6. Open the model so that both triangles (the whole mountain) are revealed above a rectangle.

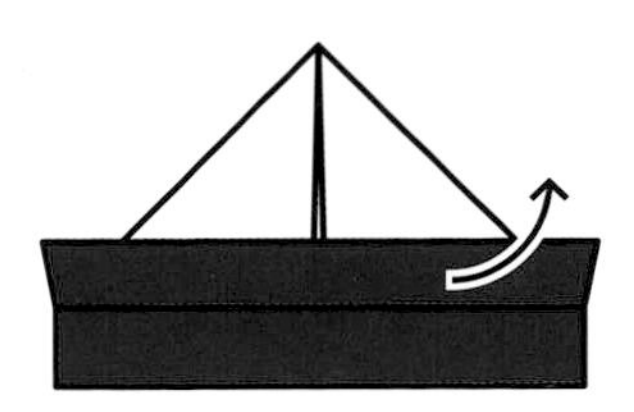

7. Fold the top rectangle flap upward (go through the valley).

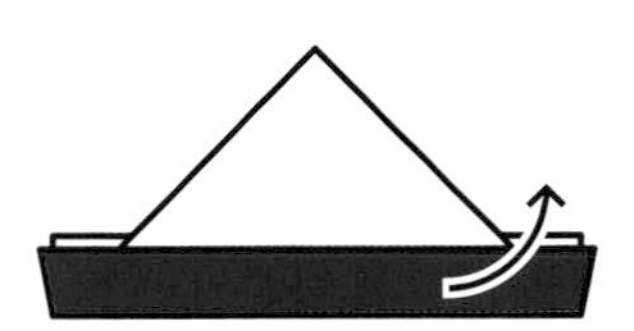

8. Turn the model over. Fold the rectangle flap upward (go through another valley).

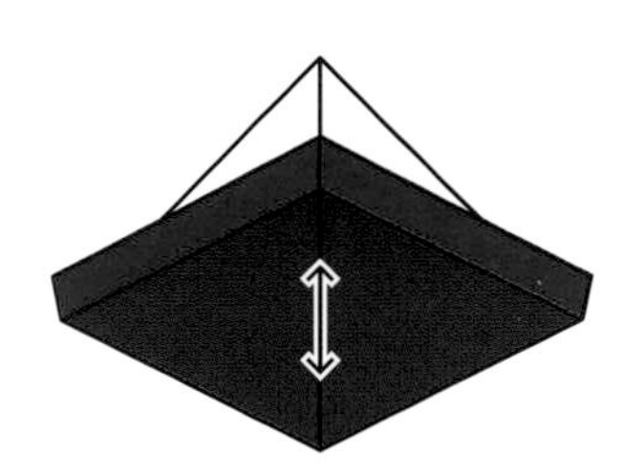

9. Open the bottom of the model — try on your hat!

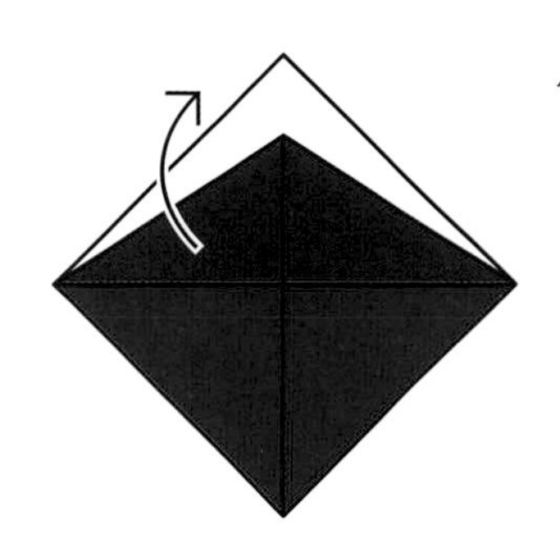

11. With the opening toward you, fold the top flap up into a triangle (trip on a rock), lining up its point with the top of the diamond.

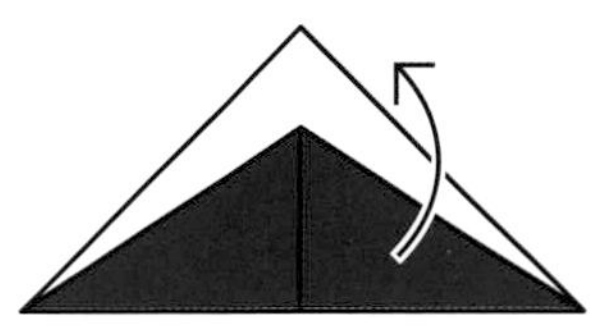

12. Turn the model over. Fold the flap up into a triangle (trip on another rock), lining up its point with the top of the other triangle.

10. Open the bottom of the model all the way. Next, rotate it so the points face you (the cave entrance). Then flatten it into a diamond, tucking in the flap corners.

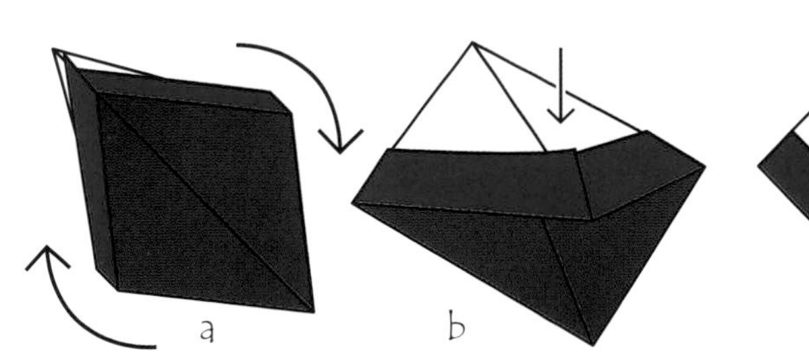


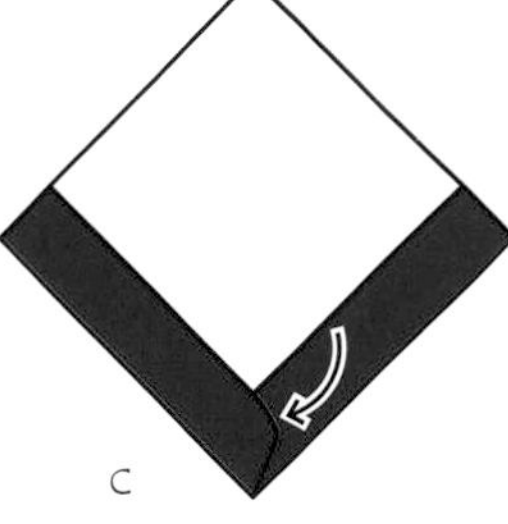


13. Open the bottom of the model (the cave exit). Next, rotate it so the points face you. Then flatten it into a smaller diamond.

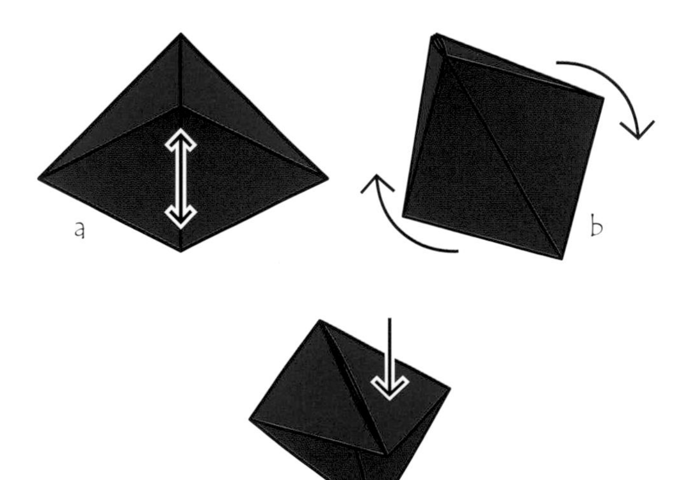

14. Pull the tips at the top of the diamond outward — it's a boat!

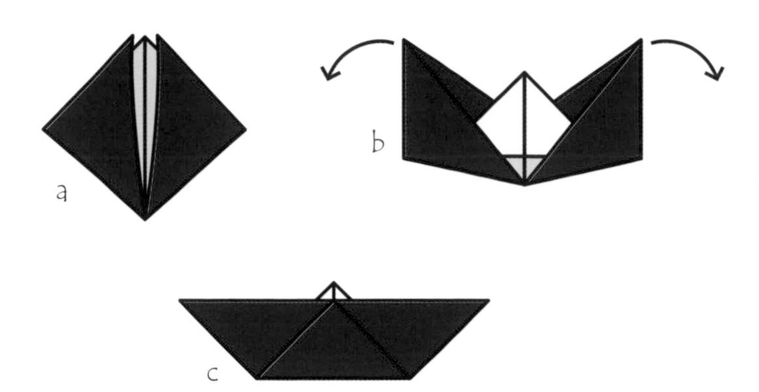


15. Tear or cut off the tip of the triangle in the middle of the boat. (Lightning strikes!)

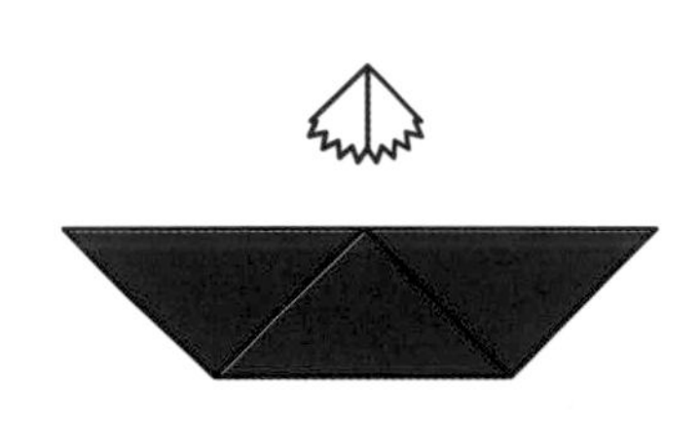

16. Tear or cut off one end of the boat up to the bottom corner. (Shark attack!)

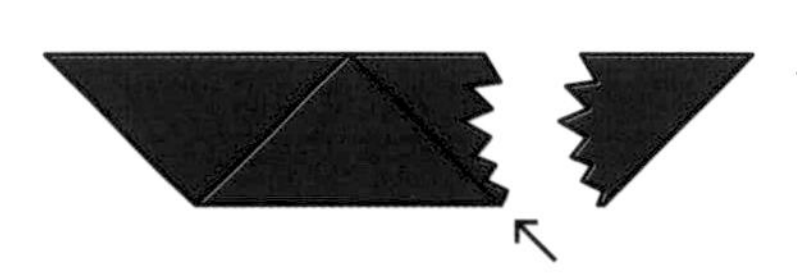

17. Tear or cut off the other end of the boat. (Shipwreck!)

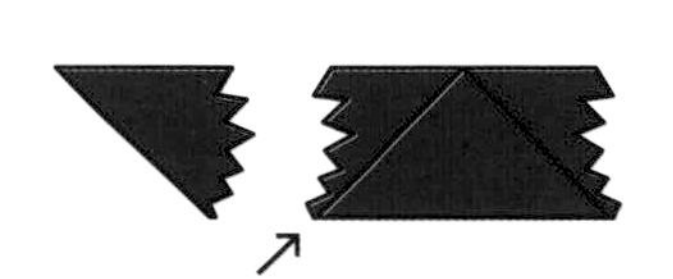

18. Unfold the sides of the boat downward (the treasure bundle). Unfold them again.

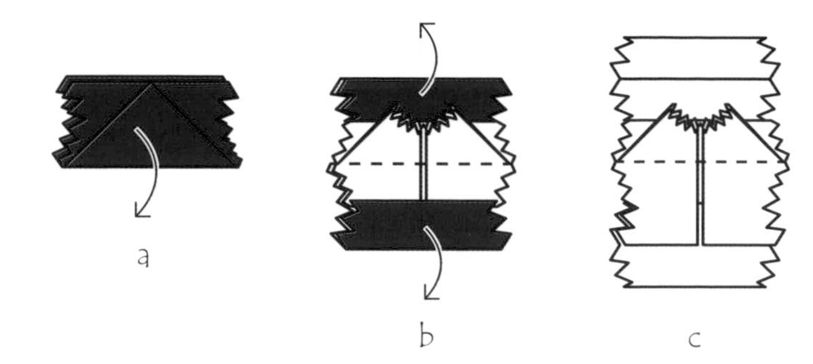


19. Unfold the left and right flaps outward, flattening the back flap at the same time — it's your own origami pirate's shirt!

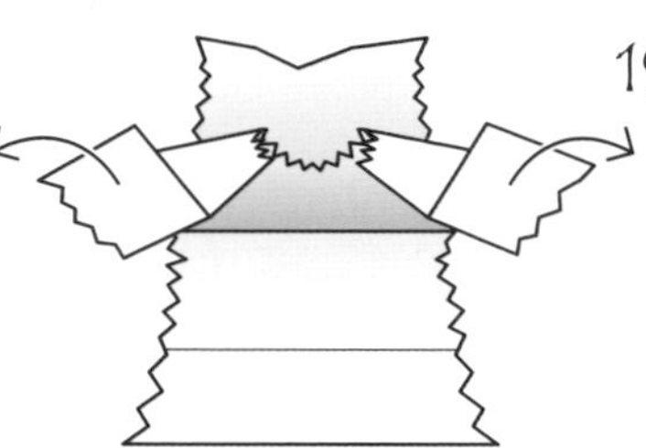

Now have fun telling your friends and family the story and making all sorts of paper treasure — hats, boats and shirts!